ARANYAKA

Celebrating
30 Years of Publishing
in India

AMRUTA PATIL

ARANYAKA

with

DEVDUTT PATTANAIK

HarperCollins *Publishers* India

First published in India in 2019
First published by HarperCollins Publishers 2023
4th Floor, Tower A, Building No 10, DLF Cyber City, DLF Phase II,
Gurugram – 122002 www.harpercollins.co.in

2 4 6 8 10 9 7 5 3 1

P-ISBN: 978-93-5699-347-1
E-ISBN: 978-93-5699-348-8

Printed and bound at
Thomson Press (India) Ltd

FOREST

I am Katyayani the Large. The warp of my story has always been hunger.

It was, at first, a world with no life on it. Forms emerged from forces of earth, wind, water and fire. There was no witness and no one to keep time. And it was a world without appetite.

The clouds moved, but not towards food.
Fire has something that resembles appetite. It does not fight to survive though.

Maybe time slid slowly, maybe time slid fast. There wasn't anyone there to measure. In a sludge of soil and water, there was frisson – so we are told. But who knows? Who really knows? Even the gods came later.
Something stirred. A scintilla, hungry.

More scintilla emerged. Some huddled together, wrapped themselves in membrane. Now they were a unit, separate from those that moved on the outside.
Inside this membrane is Us. Beyond the membrane, Them.
We can eat Them. But they must not eat Us.
The origin of tribes is this.

Everything grew urgently hungry. The wide-open maw of life demanded to be fed.

Most creatures who can't move, feed on the elements.
Most creatures who move, feed on the unmoving –
– and on other creatures who move.

To eat is to stave off death. To kill is to stave off death for a while. To reproduce is to stave off death in futures to come.
Within each living scintilla, there is great fidelity to life, and great reluctance to die. In aranya, there is great violence, but no violation.
At the moment of its death, the eyes of your prey register terror, but not accusation.

Within this dense forest and its fringes, every known drama unfolds.
Are you predator? Then I must fear you, outrun you.
Are you prey? Then I must kill and eat you.

Are you my rival? Then I must fight and subdue you, or cede passage.
Are you ally? Then I must give you something, to get what I need.

I was born in a village four valleys away. We fed off aranya. We would not let aranya feed on us. We were humans. We chose to be ants in the anthill, bees in the beehive – settlements for those who obeyed without question.

No part of me is restrained enough to meet a hive's approval. My siblings, cousins, neighbours – rule-followers, all – have an indemnity that could never be mine. My father is a learned man, a great man. As his daughter, the burden of propriety is on me. It sits there awkwardly.

For me, life is a cherry tree in a good year – bent with fruit succulent to bursting point. Wait too long, and all the fruit could rot overnight.
Detach here, so the tree doesn't pump food into beheaded stalks.
There! Hiding and eating all by herself!
Eating alone has no charm. I'd risk my life crawling up skinny branches to get cherries for others if they had wanted anything but to shame me. My appetite was bottomless, they said, my stomach grotesque. I was Katyayani the Large.
Have mercy on those branches.
My appetite felt just about right to me.

Food was regulated, roles were regulated.
The day I ate food offered to the gods, I finally went too far.
This is a stone! It has no mouth!
I'm alive! I'm hungry! Who needs food more?
The goddess has eyes. You don't see her, but she sees you.
Throw her out!
Exile was inevitable.

Hive creatures ejected from the matrix are as good as dead. Made soft by reliable food supply and controlled clime, they do not know how to survive the world outside.

My mother protested and wept at my eviction, but my father submitted to the will of the hive. They reassured my mother that a change would do me good.

Forest lore makes aranya seem clawless and affable, with a human lord-master who tames all chaos while bright-eyed faunae sing his praise.
The treeline leading towards aranya is like a hair trail that plunges into the dark chevron of sex. The closer I got, the faster my confidence ebbed.

Countless life forms stirred, most invisible to my eyes. Eliminate the visible, and the invisible still remains. In those shadows that swallowed light, I was no longer the Large – I was Katyayani the Insignificant.

I was so unprepared for this. But if you can withstand the blows and not cry foul at every adventure gone wrong, aranya opens itself to you.

I crawled out of my hiding place only when the hunger became unbearable. A forest dresses richly, but is less eager to feed than it would appear. Food is hard to come by, and water even more so. Yet, most of aranya lacks the imagination to be fearful about tomorrow's hunger and thirst.

Big cats only carry enough in their belly to last till the next kill. Elephants do remember scarcity, but they don't hoard – instead, they rely on an elder to be the keeper of collective memory.

I found the pursuit of water more nerve-racking than that of food, because it's so hard to stockpile. I looked to trees for clues to where water may lie close. Two-headed palms. Clusters of varied species. Trunks with a bulging base.
The tussle between animals is visible.
But even seemingly inert trees engage in violent combat.
Above ground, they jostle and strategise for light. Below ground, for water and minerals. Some neighbours they compete with. Others become allies.

Aranya hedges her bets. In many forms of life, instinct for sex overrides instinct for survival. A male bee literally sacrifices his endophallus at the altar of sex.

It wasn't long before I learned the way of aranya: You eat. You get eaten. You fight, often unto death, to preserve turf and to get the best mate. Human laws are meaningless here. Aranya doesn't mind you alive, it doesn't mind you dead. In fact, it doesn't care one way or the other. Here, I wasn't Katyayani the Large, but predator, prey, ally, rival, mate.

The unsolitary can run with the herd or hunt with the pack. The pack pursues its food with agile limb and unsheathed claw. The herd runs fast and kicks hard to escape death. Only the fit and the fortunate survive, hopefully with a full stomach. Until hunger rises again.

Only someone who has never known real hunger will make villains of all predators and victims of all prey.

The odds aren't great for making it alive through aranya without a teacher. This wasn't the tame, tested vegetation of my mother's garden. I had grazed the cheek of death often – starving, sick to the gut from a bad choice. It made me do things my father would never have approved of.

An animal that makes it through a day alive and fed does not bow in gratitude. A human, at the end of a harrowing day, is quite likely to give thanks to the large tree that gave food, the cave that gave refuge. Aranya has no need for thanks. The need to believe that someone cares is purely human.
You see my fears. You offer me relief.
The origins of old gods are these.

OTHERS

In human settlements, the best way to be safe is to threaten no one. Low light and low visibility make you imagine things: anthromorphs, zoomorphs, monsters as hairy as your fears. With no one to watch your back, an animal's run of the forest floor is short. A good strategy is to have deadly spines and sharp teeth, armour that's impenetrable. Even better is to melt into the backdrop with camouflage.

'Show me your real face' is a cry to disarm, more than what most people are willing to offer.

I began to paint myself to be more invisible or daunting. My old clothes were replaced by strips of beaten bark, pelts of dead animals. I rubbed my skin with animal fat to mask clues of my fear and my sex. As I grew more confident, I began to wear twigs and shells, flowers and intertwined vines. The beginnings of adornment are these: The less I cowered from my surroundings, the more I began to play.

Solitude is okay, but I am not a loner. I'm happy to be carried awhile on wide, loving shoulders in exchange for a fistful of berries. Clawless, fangless humans survive aranya by imitating strategies of other species. Like insects who carry pollen for flowers in exchange for nectar or like geese sharing navigation and vigil duty during migratory flight.

I met all sorts. Generous people, people who took more than their share, people who hurt others, people who stole. We learn tricksy things from other species. Some male spiders offer a silk-wrapped package to a female just before mounting her for sex. Sometimes the gift contains a juicy fly, sometimes a withered corpse. Sometimes the parcel is empty, a total hoax.

A male who has finished copulating
may snatch his gift back and make a run for it,
to offer the same gift to another female,
for another shot at copulation. Like
I said, all sorts.

Fear demands the comfort of intimacy. Collaborators huddle to kindle fires to dispel scary shadows. Together, we gathered fruit and speared fish.
We led one another to safe cave systems.
These liaisons changed the way I lived, the way I ate.

Some left me offerings of food. Will they return? Will there be food tomorrow? I kept reserves buried, tucked away in crevices for future hungers. Those who can't imagine tomorrow's hunger must forage without respite.

I did not cling to my collaborators, nor they to me. Seasoned to autonomy, we shared generously but travelled light.
We were birds resting in the middle of the ocean to break a long journey.
Companions till dawn.

My father taught us to be careful with termite mounds. We had heard of the princess who tried to reach what she thought were fireflies in one and ended up gouging the eyeballs of the sage inside. I came across a man in a termite mound one day – immutable, oblivious to insect bites, hunger pangs, scorching sun – but his eyes were not as bright as fireflies yet.
What are you doing?
Watching the world.
Then how come you don't see the tasty food before you?

He had a longwinded name, but I only ever called him Y – name as query! Y didn't covet me. He looked at me investigatively, like a botanist encountering unknown taxa. I, on the other hand, wanted to consume him immediately.
Let me kiss you.
My next instinct was to feed him.
Kiss me! Taste me! Enjoy me!
Was I the seductress my mother used to speak of?

Fire of hunger, fat of love, water to sate the burn – this is the stuff of which intimacies are forged. I could chart the forest by where we ate and where we made love. We feasted and rested, rested and feasted, moving only to gather appetite and ingredients for our next feast.

The herd that Y 'chose' to leave was his teacher's.

His teacher was the Great Ritualist, master of elaborate systems. He taught his students the codes of yagna, down to their minutiae. On the Ritualist's turf, this was this and that was that, and that was it. Everything was measured.

Gesture of offering to the gods – To family – To yourself – To forefathers –

We fear simple explanations; offerings are food for the hungry, hunger is exchange of food between humans and gods.

Y regurgitated all the knowledge he had acquired. So tidy was his vomit, fellow students became partridges and swallowed it. By ingesting a part of Y, they hoped they'd see the world as he did.

Y felt the Ritualist was an insecure man who knew less than he claimed. Disappointed with all human teachers, he walked off to witness aranya.

Y walked into the forest. Terror followed. All the skills he had learned from the Ritualist were totally useless here. The deeper he ventured, the harder it became to see the sun he had sworn to follow. Still, he persisted.
The sun does not teach. It is we who are convinced it illuminates us.
O Sun, you were my original Herring Gull mother.
Others were sticks with red dots I mindlessly followed.

In aranya's low light, Y soothed his fears by collecting data and finding patterns. He observed astutely, strategised carefully and interacted minimally.

Occasionally he merged forces with other loners to collaborate on a big kill that would keep everyone fed for weeks.

The forest as Y knew it was so different from the forest I knew. I observed to engage and enjoy. He observed to withdraw – and detach.

To me, the night sky was delightfully unfamiliar – countless pinpricks of light. Y got a raging headache if he couldn't divide up the sky into constellations.
There are so many different ways a river may be crossed.
The boulder configurations Y and I chose were different, but we were equally adept at traversing.
Mine was a gut-know, deep and mute. His was probability, statistics and math. Our different maps of the world came together to make a rich atlas.

Everything in the forest is sex-encrusted. Sprayed pheromone on bark. Pollen and spore. Bawdiness of unfurled flowers. Even the rot is sweet and full of promise. There is no kind of rutting you will not see here. Long-term coupling. Pair-bonding. Homosexuality. Coercive sex. Inter-species sex. Group assault. Nothing can startle those who have been attentive in aranya.
Our union was neither seasonal nor involuntary. I sought it. Y accepted it.

I smelled of me, of animals whose hides I wrapped around me. Y smelled of sweat, smoke, petrichor. I made towards him like wild animals to a salt lick.
If your smell changes, I'll have to leave you.
And what if our appetites change?

Y was not the most attentive or resourceful of men. Nor the strongest, the best-endowed, most libidinous or romantic. He was the cleverest though, and the most hungry learner. But once every cranny and orifice of our feasting had been probed, he began to get restless and sought escape.
Before we met I lived on sunlight and not much else.
It cannot have been fun.
This gluttony is making me soft.
Rip your stomach out and get done with it?
I laughed, but with pain and foreboding in my heart.

Y didn't rip out his stomach, he rejected it. Everything that wasn't utilitarian began to annoy him, distract him. He rejected pleasure and play. Aranya became a fetter. I knew he was far gone when he lost his startle response.
You can't do this in a forest! You can't leave your back exposed!
I need focus and stillness!
The luxury of stillness isn't for hunter-gatherers. Leaving had become inevitable.

FIELD

You can kill a tree unsubtly or subtly. You can over-water it till the roots rot, or starve it slowly. You can kill it with flame or axe or poison at the roots.

We went from suckling at the Great Mother's teat to lacerating her breast. Hundreds of trees were beheaded and burned to make our field. Countless micro-habitats destroyed. Soil hidden for millennia was laid bare.
May our blade never cause you lingering pain.
The origins of settlement are these.

Filled with remorse after clearing the field, I ran back to the forest and ate the fruit of the largest banyan tree. All of aranya seemed to rumble and stir inside my belly. I knew then that the field would rejuvenate after the destruction.

Before the tree, there was a seed. After the tree, there is a seed. The circularity of life. From now on – end of equality – we would decide what was crop and what was weed.

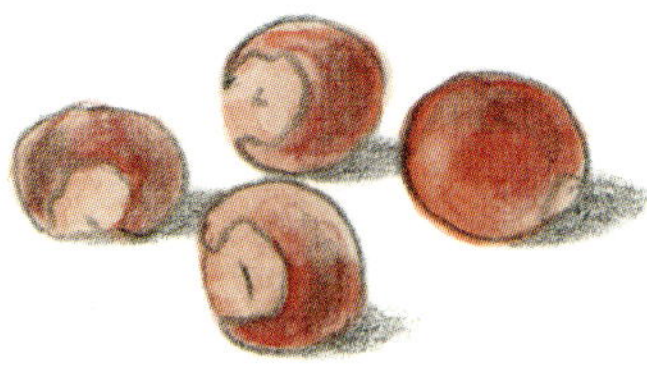

Did I mention I was pregnant? One seed was sown, now we'd sow others. I had brought seeds of my favourite plants from the forest. I pressed them into the exposed soil. The earth offered no resistance. The tulsi was planted at what would be the entrance to our home – her fragrance a reminder of aranya, her thirst a reminder of hunger.

I dressed for utility and safety in the forest. Strategically dowdy, unless the aim was to be daunting. Things were different in the field. Here, colours of wings and petals flashed and burned. They did not fear display, mostly.

Security and the fallow season changed my own adornments.

Aesthetically, I came into my own on the field.

Season after season, we waited upon the same patch of land. There were details I knew from having returned to the site over and over. Aranya gave me some of her secrets, but a farmer knows things a wanderer never will.

We worked hard. Rules slowly came into being. Tasks were clearly defined, evenly distributed, tidily executed. I fed the earth with as much care as I did my beloved. Each head of corn had a fish head at its roots.

We had exchanged sounds of the forest for songs of the field.

Membranes formed. The first separated the field from aranya.

The second membrane enclosed the courtyard, separating Y's world from mine.

Y and I had three babies on the field.
To my firstborn, I was feline mother, carrying the babe safe but immobilised. To my second, I was monkey mother, trusting the infant's instinct to hold on.
I was turtle mother to the third, burying the egg and leaving it to its fate.
By forest norms, Y and I had outsmarted the Big Death. Few couples stay joined at the hip afterwards. Why did I think we'd fare differently?

Those who had known me in aranya were disappointed with how my life looked on the field. They thought me stunted and enslaved. They thought I had lost my teeth. But then they also imagined all birds to be constantly migratory. If only they knew the unambitious trajectories of most.

To cloister at night the cattle you look after by day –

To be unfettered and voluntarily feed others: this is love, not servitude.

Y took his time becoming. The cells of giant trees grow very slowly – their own mothers will restrict light so the young don't shoot up too fast. In Y's sprawl, saplings would thrive. Our children basked in his attention and love.

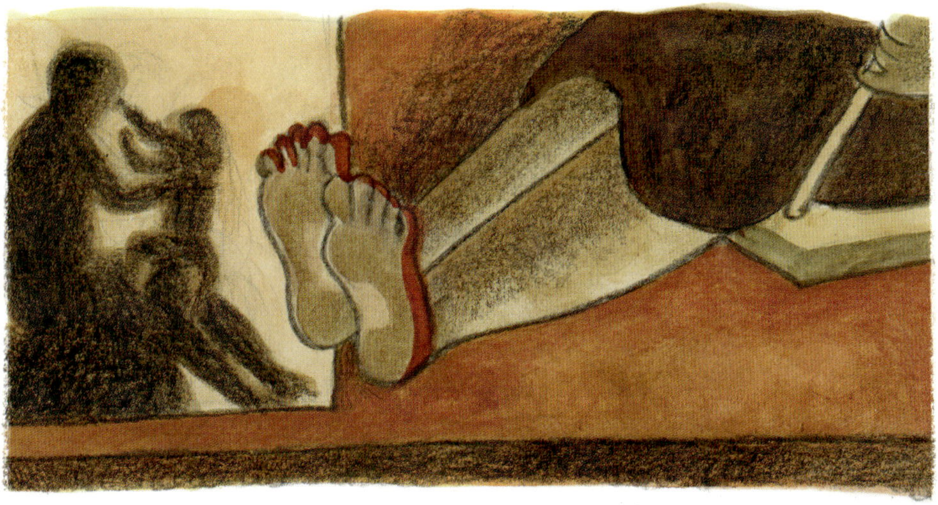

The nurturing father now attained the gravitas of a teacher. A magisterial new quality alighted on Y. He surfaced, magnificent as the sun.

Those who frowned at my domestication were overwhelmed by Y's effulgence and were ready to be his students. Only I knew the young man in the termite mound.

The seed was not of my making, but I did ensure the soil wasn't too rocky and no louche grazers caused damage. That there was enough water but not so much the roots would rot, there was shade when shade was needed, and no untimely frost or caterpillars. I dreaded the inevitable arrival of greatness.

A banyan tree is not a friend of households. Under it gather the detached and unrooted, the seekers, the traders, the ghouls and wanderers.

A whale doesn't ask a lamprey to suck on its flesh. Y didn't ask for others to turn up in our field. But he soon grew habituated to their presence. If you are a large animal, you become an ecosystem that feeds others.

If you are miserly, the system will leech off you anyway.

Almost anyone you encounter in aranya is there because of merit and a measure of luck. Weaklings don't survive long enough to lay claim to food or mate. The field, however, doesn't care for merit. If the harvest is abundant, even the runt of the litter will be taken care of.

First to arrive here were those looking to collaborate – those who sought a missing piece in their puzzle offered another in exchange. When Y's puzzle began completing itself, the collaborators were replaced by seekers. Collaborators were allies, seekers predators. They hated one another.

Often young and fragile, seekers looked for comfort, not clarity. They frowned upon collaborators as disrespectful and too-familiar around the teacher. Collaborators, in turn, saw them as lazy and inept.

Systems began to run smoothly. Everyone had a role. Together we removed weeds, planted crops, checked pests. A healthy ecosystem did the rest.

Only one collaborator came to Y's fold in the later years: the Weaver. She could've been his equal, but she arrived too late. By then, Y did not want collaborators anymore. He wanted disciples.

Unlike me, the seekers sought gravitas, not play from Y.

They grazed like cattle on the wordy pastures of Y. They inhabited the metaphor of aranya with greater ease than they could ever inhabit a real forest. In fact, they talked ceaselessly about the world as a way to avoid really living in it.

As a young man, Y dismissed all teachers to follow the sun. In his middle age, he was oddly complicit in letting others anoint him sun. He took his role seriously. A guru is both mother and father – and Y felt parental guilt at being more fond of some wards than others.

Three babies have sucked my teats, not all made my heart fond to exactly the same degree. Peach trees need different attention than prickly pears. Given the same treatment, one will die.

They came in a steady stream and lingered for days, weeks, months. What was in our granary fed everyone who came by. My kitchen nurtured the very classroom that took Y away from me.

We strove for abundance and the earth provided: enough for the farmer, enough for a thief! I stood by Y's side in welcome and goodbye.
I returned to the kitchen when the discourse began.
You should join us here, Katyayani.
Who will feed us then?
Besides, the hair-splitting really bored me.

Y tried to convince me to join the classroom. My ignorance had now become an embarrassment. A membrane formed between Y and I, between his side and my side.
There's more to the world than cowpats and stirring pots!
If everyone is busy with prayer and philosophy, who will plant the potatoes?
I had grown bodily larger since aranya, but somehow, the bigger I got, the more invisible I seemed to become to those around me.

If his teacher was the Great Ritualist, Y was the Great Rejector. Rejecting teachers, forest, collaborators, the food I was, and the food I served.

I learned to use firesticks to light a fire long ago. Fires in a forest need to be put out as soon as one's work is done, for safety. In my kitchen, the fire was fed constantly.

In aranya, we ate quicky before some other animal got to the food. Here, there was no rush or danger. We ate at fixed intervals, unprompted by pangs of hunger.

Bored palettes must be teased awake. I learned alchemy in the kitchen: flavours, textures, temperatures. The exact moment when potatoes soften in their jackets and ooze –

– aromatic roots sizzle in ghee and release a fragrance sublime –

– and steamed turmeric leaf starts yielding its essence to the flesh of river fish.

We emerged at meal times, our procession almost ceremonial.
We competed for attention, a good-natured sport. Y worked to ensure the discussions were so juicy, no one would remember lunch. I worked to ensure there was no way they could resist. When aromas hit the mark, eyes darted towards the steaming pots. Debates about duality and non-duality came to a standtill. Y shook his head in mock despair –
Session's over. Time to eat.
You can't philosophise on a hungry belly.

The cause of suffering is hunger, said Y. I dealt with it by rustling up a great feast. Y dealt with it by trying to conquer his stomach and cravings.
Possible for us to eat more simply? The students can't keep awake after lunch –
The food looks fine to me.
They're here for bigger things –
Too superior for their own stomachs.

Have you ever fed anyone else voluntarily? You are welcome to eat dust or forage!
People could help if you relaxed your death-grip on that kitchen.
Life would go on –
The cruelty of this.
And the cruelty of making people eat what their bodies don't need and can't digest?
...

You like my bodily presence, but you don't understand or respect what I do –
You never come to the classroom, even to listen!
Katyayani, I don't need or want so much. Why does this detail not matter to you?

You've taken more from me than you know – my space, my autonomy.
Who or what is it that you're really feeding?
Sure you're speaking about my kitchen and not your classroom?

I declared the kitchen closed until further notice. For the next three days, no one ate anything that had come in contact with fire.

But the questions Y had angrily asked would continue to haunt me. Who and what was I feeding? In my unseeing enthusiasm, the constipated were fed cherries and the flatulent ate cabbage. Many got third helpings they did not want.

I began to slip away to aranya on the days the kitchen was closed. There I learned to find pleasure anew. On my first night out, I saw the luxuriant tree cover I had seen countless times before. For the first time, I noticed the care trees took to ensure their canopies didn't touch one another.
Each searching for the best light, but giving the others space.
Together, but apart.

You look so happy here. Are you sure you want the field or Y at all?
I like being here knowing I can return to a dry bed, a stocked kitchen.
And I love him.
Why does Y want you?
He loves me too, but in his own way.
I chose to bring a bit of aranya back home. The beginning of my grove was this.

GROVE

The most common thing about a field is an enclosure, often rectangular, sign of ownership and control. What lies within this enclosed membrane is 'mine'. What lies outside is 'not mine'. Outsiders may not enter without permission.
My grove
My kitchen
Our field
Our cows
Our courtyard
Thoughts, too, are rectangular here.
Y's classroom
Banyan tree, aranya beyond
They take a world of complex edges, break it into constituent bits so there is no wild whole to fear. Meat that's minced can't be a whole goat again.

Clay was still my medium. I didn't paint my face or body with it anymore. Instead, I kneaded and coaxed it as I might a lover's flesh. I wet and patted it, coiled it, smoothed and raised it. I shaped it to enclose a piece of sky.

Earth, water and an oven's womb come together in the making of earthen pots.

The purnakumbha, brimming with water, marks a new membrane. On that side, the field. On this side, the grove: aranya in microcosm. On that side, staple crop and no weeds. Here, no fence, no hedge, no flower bed.
I planted by my nose and my eyes joined the feast: things that roused, calmed, healed. But a lot grew here that was never planted by human hand.

Trees had been my reference point in aranya. There was nothing altruistic about them. Contrary to what people think, a fruiting tree is a bad analogy for selflessness. Being irresistible is part of its survival plan.

At the farthest end of the grove is the killing block. Y rejected it because he didn't want to eat death anymore. If he knew how many creatures had to be terminated for each meal that reached his plantain leaf!
Food demands violence, but violence is terrifying. Every part of a felled tree and culled animal satisfies a need.

We were as different as sky and earth. Our equation was once of shared activity – foraging, sex, travel, keeping vigil. The field brought a new sensation: stillness. When the toil was over, we followed clouds with our eyes, punctuated the stillness with stories we knew.

The stories from the forest – odes to rock, water, fire, thunder – became remote and fell into disuse. Our lives were different now. In the new stories, animals true to their forest-nature gave way to vainglorious peacocks and cowardly chickens, avaricous jackals, cruel lions, jealous foxes. They were 'bird' or 'animal' only in caricatured form. Other stories turned them into gods.

These stories emerged to explain a changing world., new gods better suited to the enclosed rectangles and full pots of the field. Some gods were braves who guarded livestock, grain, gold, progeny. Others took away uncertainty.
On the hood of a snake is a red jewel that brings fortune.
At night, the rope looked like a snake.
Aranya's creatures turned into codes on my walls –
Fertility
Abundance
Protection

The more I saw, the more I knew how little they saw me. They who valued scholarship and bodily restraint above all, what did they make of me? Big, greedy woman? Guru's unlettered wife? Skilful kitchen hand?
Do you see me?
Their eyes glazed over without malice. No, they didn't see me at all.

My natural kinship is with village goddesses of lidless, staring eyes. Like me, they are simple women, simpletons even. Their reflexes, like mine, are unsophisticated – quick to curse and forgive, generous with food and love. Never above a tantrum or jealous, piping-hot rage.

If I gave you the impression that I inhabited invisibility with grace, I haven't told you enough. I hated Y's students. Many were like spring's ephemeral flowers – brazenly needy, desperate to impress, no passing insect left unseduced. Such was their haste that some did not distinguish between a fidel, picky honeybee –

It's tempting to judge ephemerals for their neediness, but their time in the sun is so short. Flowers of long life can afford to be picky. The more I learned to see Y's followers as creatures of aranya, the less threatening they became. The traits of birds and beasts are written large in human beings.

Humans, like animals, have two things in common: they are hungry and full of fear. I saw how different creatures must be approached –

Crouching at eye level or coyly avoiding any eye contact.

Authoritatively, with big gestures, making oneself larger than one is.

To his growing despair, Y found himself spending more and more time handling the friction amongst the growing entourage of seekers.

And he did.
When you open your eyes as wide as the gods' –
– you see humans in aranya and aranya in humans. That's all.
I showed Y the mundane and the magical faces of my garden.
Hard outside, soft inside
Quick to bristle
Sour
Piquant
Untouched by the mire
Jumpy
Unwilling to be pinned down

There was a pleasing quality to how Y paid attention when he did. A silky focus reserved for those who told him what he did not already know. Seekers sifted river beds for that one gold nugget that would make Y silky.
He was fascinated by the data I had gathered.
<< Green fingers, extension of a verdant heart. >>
<< Bloom where you're planted. >>
This is incredible.
My garden was full of reflections and Y stopped by frequently to look.

They made their way into Y's philosophical discourse.

I thought we were equals,
bilateral symmetry of leaves.
He, fire of
enlightenment.
And me, fire of
the microcosm.
Y thought we were
halves, not equals.
He, above.
Me, below.

RIVALS

Y's way was to assert via negation. Negate bonds, negate the senses, negate all desires. Not this, not that – until you transcend limitations of space, time, language, and unite with the limitless universe.

My way is to affirm and connect. This too, that too – cycles, seasons, passage of time, melody of language. When I first met Y, he shunned all stimuli, neither seeking food, nor offering any.

In Y's classroom, he did not distinguish between genders or stratas of society. They were all minds here. They reminded me of the Atlas moth. Born without a mouth, it burns its own body fat while it searches for a mate. Then it mates, and dies.
To me, no fate is more horrific than to be stuck in a mouthless body.
Y deflected these moths from his fire to mine.
First to come my way was Upakoshala, called 'Uppi' by all.

Uppi was attentive to a fault, thoughtful and wise. The sight of me gutting a pile of roundfish made him flinch. He was apologetic about his revulsion. I reminded him of his butcher wife, gleeful with her sharp blades and blood-streaked apron – the one he walked away from at night without any warning or address.

I sent him off beyond the field with the cows. The cows didn't really need him, he needed them. At dusk, they would walk him back, safe and sound.

You can hunt deer or hare or go hungry. But I cannot let you take my teacher's cows.
You seemed like a fair man. But there's a hierarchy in your head about which lives matter and which don't –
Take my life then, and sate your hunger. Spare the cows.
You're burned by tapas, I can't eat you. Go, your cows are safe. Spare a thought for the oxen, castrated by a farmer's blade.
All the way home, Uppi was restless.

When he returned to the field, he threw himself at my feet in gratitude.

I had no idea what he was talking about or who Satyakama Jabali was. My only intention had been to get Uppi out of my hair. It was all quite confusing.

Y took Uppi's departure as a personal failure, a slight.
His resolve was weak. We have lost Upakoshala to an internship in the kitchen.
We fast for two days. You can eat fruit off the ground, raw tubers –
I thought of Uppi and the charm of the four words he had left in my palm.
'She is not me.'
It permanently altered my parameters of seeing. It changed my eyes.
'He is not me.'
Why do I judge him for not being me?

I wondered if I had only been feeding those who laughed at the same jokes as I did, whose faces were matching full moons, bellies as convex as mine. Would I be able to feed someone who did not resemble me?
Isn't she beautiful and interesting? I may ask her to eat with me one day.
That's your reflection you're looking at!
One day, the Weaver arrived with her dogs and a loom. Her reputation as a scholar preceded her. Y asked that the dogs remain outside the field. Their worship of her annoyed him.
They waited, eyes boring into her back even when she was out of sight.

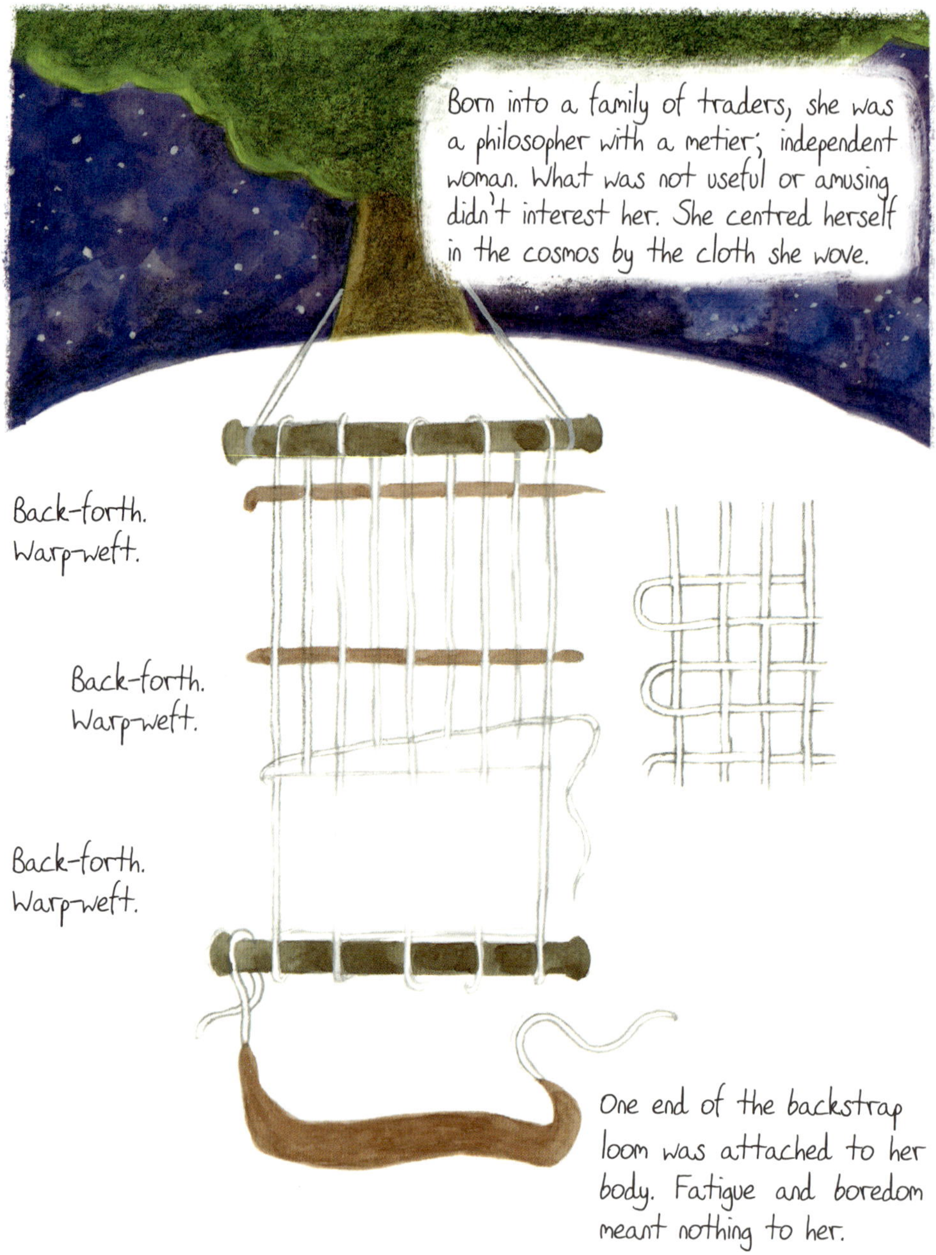

The Weaver's doggedness was the warp around which complex ideas knotted themselves. For fabric to be resilient, the warp threads on the loom must be strong and under great tension. Around warp, weft dances whimsical and delicate.

From the very first day she sat legs outstretched in Y's direction, the Weaver was a polarising presence. The placement of her legs was a practical choice so she could rest her loom. But fellow students to whom respect meant sitting motionless and opinion-free as a corpse found the posture unacceptable. Y could not care less. He only saw her mind.

The Weaver had never met a teacher confident enough to allow a student to surpass him. She hungered to be crowned by the best. She felt Y could be the one. For his part, Y was quite taken with the Weaver.

The Weaver could have been heir to Y's knowledge. But she wanted to go beyond. She saw agreement as submission and defeat.

She was sent to my kitchen and I observed her carefully. Among birds, she would be a woodpecker hammering at a mark until the most unyielding of hard places was pierced – persistent beak absorbing the impact so the brain didn't suffer.

Among plants, she would be the groundnut, a species that simply won't trust others to do a job as well as it can. When pollination is done and the fruits ripe, it will bend over, plant its own seed in the soil.

Among animals, she'd be a snail, hermaphrodite whose male body part will dally with many, but whose female receptacle is extraordinarily picky.

For all that she was given, the Weaver paid back in exact measure. She had a horror of debt. Like all traders, she had an uncanny ability to read people and their desires. This wasn't out of generosity, it was because she thought it fair.

A good transaction must leave both parties sated. Back-forth. Warp-weft.

My hair terrified and distracted her. The weaver in her had a great desire to tame flyaway filaments. She offered me a smooth, beautiful comb.
Your loose hairs might fall into the food you cook –
Braiding my hair is out of the question. Even a clean centre-parting is hard to pull off.
You don't like this, do you?
Her revulsion only made me hairier. My hair broke her comb. In fact, it would go on to break all the combs she tried to control it with.

Like my hair, aranya terrified the Weaver – it resisted tidy partings. Y had charted all the rivers and valleys in the forest to comfort himself. The Weaver, on the other hand, mapped every way to avoid entering a forest.
But like all animals, she saw only opportunity or threat.
What are his strengths and weaknesses?
Is this competition?
Is this collaboration?

The Weaver was an effective cook, but not very efficient. She made what she knew and she made it well. She sought the quickest way from chopping block to pot – which often meant a lot of wastage.

Two-fifths of each okra was lopped off.

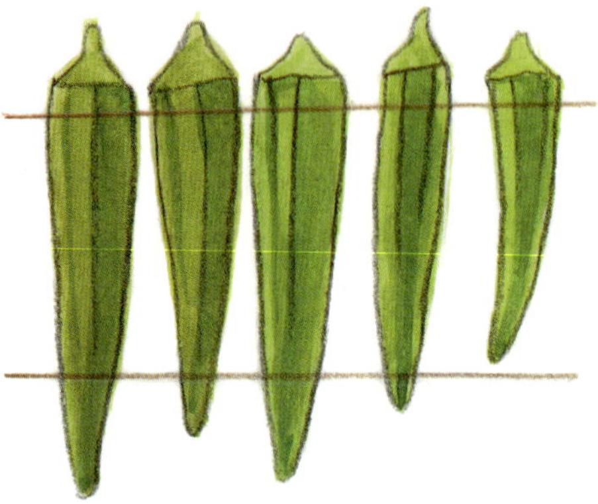

Two-fifths of each fish was thrown away.

Her favourite kitchen implement was a grinding stone on which resistance was broken, truth extracted from grain, seed and fibre. Unlike other seekers, the Weaver did not shirk work in the kitchen. She neither glorified nor shunned it.

An alchemical dance was what she did with dye and mordant too.

For the food she ate and the lessons she learned at my fire, the Weaver felt I had not been fairly remunerated. The broken combs weighed on her.

She pulled out a pouch full of dry cochineal beetles collected off cactii far away. She crushed and dissolved them in water. Alum and lime brought about an explosion of purple, rich as the loveliest orchids or grape stains. She was pleased to see my delight – it was a successful transaction.

It was truly the most sublime purple I had seen. It made me so happy, I never wore another colour again. We talked about the Weaver's way, of paying off debt to rid herself of obligation. She felt I was just like her, spending so much time in the kitchen, cooking for others to shrug off the burden of debt.

She worked it matter-of-factly, the loom she did not choose. Needless to say, the Weaver excelled at her work. Of all threadbearers, she liked spiders the most. Unlike silkworms, their spinning didn't end as a death song in boiling water.

It was while trading cloth in the marketplace that the Weaver refined her understanding of measurement, exchange, bargain – and human character.

On the Weaver's loom, complex human behaviours and preoccupations were mapped in simplified motifs. Like the rectangles on the field, nature was articulated angularly.

Intangible – tangible
Opportunity – threat
Debt – repayment
Back – forth
Warp – weft

Y was intrigued by the Weaver's stint in my kitchen – she seemed content enough, neither overwhelmed nor transformed like Uppi had been. The Weaver, in Y's eyes, had passed some sort of test. He was relieved.

M, who came to be known as the Fig, arrived here alone and unescorted, terrifying apparition covered in soot.

When the soot came off, I hated her even more. What made this new arrival so unbearable? Her stomata and lenticels I couldn't identify.

Her foreigness was unsettling, as was the fact that she barely ate. How grotesque my gobbling and my belly-overhang must have seemed to her! When it was M's turn to cook, her estimate of what ten people ate was more suited to three.

And still the food was inadequately salted. This made me irritable.

While everyone else toiled, M was shielded from all unpleasantness, hardship, and the burning sun. So rare was her beauty and finesse, she was kept unencumbered and taught the best of the sixty-four arts. M had, in her throat, a songbird's syrinx instead of a larynx. A trophy spouse for one or many.

She painted, wove, danced and sculpted. She mastered the skill of adornment, coiffure and artful writing. All of it bored her immensely.

They saw her body, they saw her skills. No one saw her mind.

Day and night, she whittled her mind. Day and night, she starved herself until her beautiful breasts withered and her ribcage jutted out –

But still they did not see her mind. One day, M escaped in search of a teacher who would. She made herself unthreatening to the spouses of prospective teachers, so they wouldn't see her as a rival. She swam upstream like a salmon, adapting from fresh water to salty, back to fresh – unrecognisable from phase to phase.

M had tiny, graceful hands. They were hands unsuited to carrying loads, cutting wood, grinding rice or giving deep massages. They were hands meant for ruby rings, for gestures that emphasised a point well-made.

She proved to be a natural garland-maker. Flowers were gathered gently, held together by knots, unpierced by needles. My suggestion that she make garlands was a devious one. For every moment of their short, brazen lives, flowers are about sex and sex only. You don't need UV vision or compound eyes to see this.

When she was engrossed, she sang. Spontaneous lyrics from a familiar source.

There was an unerring sense of proportion about M's songs and garlands, an ability to bring together disparate imagery and herbs to splice high, sweet notes. Mogra and mint. Aboli and parsley. Marigold and mango leaf. Rose and tulsi.

Her garlands, like her analogies, were open-ended. They would generously scent your hair and body all day, but in a possessive fist they would simply wither away and perish in minutes. To know this was to know M. She herself was not a brazen flower. She resembled the subtle flowers of a fig, secret and hidden, pollination happening out of sight.

She WAS the Fig, and the name stuck.

The Fig was not me. Her aranya with its scant vegetation and rugged rockfaces had no resemblance to the dark, wet aranya I knew. She saw my forest as a source of esoteric knowledge and was curious –
Don't you miss being in the forest?
Why don't I tell you about what I do not miss?
Not knowing if I'll find a water source or if it's safe to drink.
Ticks, leeches. Wet animal hide chafing againt my raw skin.
Making a roof each time it starts raining.
Frail old people left behind as carrion-prey so a tribe doesn't lose speed.
She would've liked me to intellectualise aranya, but I couldn't. She'd have liked me to romanticise it, but I wouldn't. When you've known real danger, you don't romanticise it. You only work to avoid it.

Forest stories are mostly about men – their setbacks, triumphs. One never hears of the ill-equipped women, because those stories do not last long or end well. Rarely, one hears of aranyanis like me, women who contain aranya within them. This is what I said I missed about my old life:
The quality of light.
Looking at the moon to know the day, and the sun to know the hour.
The beauty of a human face seen after days of being lost.
The capacity of a single fallen tree to transform known topography.
What does Y think of your classroom songs?
He doesn't know there are any!
Y didn't know she made word garlands! He isn't a man stirred by listening.

The Fig skipped her secrets and songs like pebbles into loud streams.
<< The old gods and new gods and formless gods come together as tributaries. >>
<< Forest, kitchen and classroom come together as tributaries. >>
<< The Large, the Weaver and the Fig, three free-flowing rivers come together as tributaries. >>

CLASSROOM

As a man in a termite mound, Y had observed the world. As a man who outgrew both kitchen and seductress, he observed the observing eye.

As a sculptor takes on a rock face, Y took on brahman. He whittled relentlessly.

He took the Ritualist's beloved yagna and stripped it bare of ritual.
<< Don't chant what you don't understand. >>
<< The yagna, says Y, is in, and of, the body. >>
<< Your body is altar and your hunger is fire. >>
<< Food is the fuel hunger demands. >>
<< Look beyond this hunger for atman: inner fire that needs no fuel. >>
For Y, yagna connected limitless within to limitless without. Atman to brahman.

Such was Y's sadhna and focus that mediocre students simply couldn't keep pace. Over time, he only drew excellence towards himself. His was one of the most respected classrooms in the land. Y's way was this:

Y said bad arguments were about ego and delusion, good arguments brought epiphany. I felt all argument was combat. A stag with bleedy antlers is a sad sight –

The Weaver's aggression grated on Y's nerves. Brought up by doting parents, given every skill and liberty needed to survive the world, she didn't trust platitudes.

Sit still, like a rishika in a termite mound –
That isn't my learning style, Y, you know it. I learn by exchange.
<< Stop fretting the knots, Weaver! Look at the knotless fabric! >>
<< Some thirst is genuine, some questions are display. >>
<< Go beyond that discursive mind! >>

<< Go beyond! Go beyond the beyond! >>
<< Go from chatter to silence, be vast enough to accomodate infinity. >>
Vast enough to accommodate infinity, but not vast enough to accommodate a wife who has stopped short of beyond!
Tell the beyond-the-beyonds that lunch is ready. They can bring their stomachs.

My old companion the parakeet had to be exiled from my side for being indiscreet. By night, he'd pick things up; by day, he'd fly to the classroom and mimic my cries of love and spicy gossip. Now he mostly lived in the classroom and visited to tell me what he had overheard. Reverse indiscretion is indeed delightful.

Among the voices the parakeet ferried was the Weaver's. Always incisive, she no longer used complicated metaphors and abstruse lines. Instead, she spoke the unaffected language of her vocation. Back-forth. Warp-weft.

The classroom was getting too confining for the Weaver. The day wasn't far when she would take on Y. A coming-of-age duel was imminent.

For the longest time, the parakeet didn't bring me the Fig's classroom voice at all. Uninterested in being a hero or a dominator of worlds, the Fig only listened. Y and the Weaver sparred, barely listening to each other.

She was the ultimate synthesiser, alert and unseen.

The Fig's equanimity made her a popular confidante of the alphas. They mistook her quietness for complicity and fed on her receptiveness. Even Y, who thought he lived on air and pure intent, was a glutton for her attention. He gave her a special place in the class.

The Weaver always saved a place right next to her where the Fig could lay her bedding at night. To repay her for the companionship, she even wove her a drape – soft so it wouldn't chafe her skin, thick so her body's alluring contours did not show through. For the first time, the Fig received an object she really wanted. The Fig thought they saw her, but it was her adoration, not her mind they saw.

I remember the day Y gave his first public teaching about the yagna being in, and of, the human body. To disband popular ideas and suggest something so simple yet revolutionary: this was the greatness of my beloved! That night I made light, tasty, celebratory fare because Y had finally inhabited the language of the body.

Metaphor! I had been cooking for four hours. My temper flared like kindling. Body, hunger, aranya: they turned their faces from it all by making them into metaphors.

Our interaction had been overheard by the Fig standing in the shadows.

EXCHANGE

Once every twelve years, there was an immense sabha hosted by sage-king Janak. People thronged together to exchange produce, services and, most important of all, ideas. The highlight of the sabha was a philosophical debate to which the wisest minds in the land were invited. The undefeated one would go home with a generous prize.

The year our Weaver came into her own, the bounty was set at one thousand cows bedecked in gold. To a scholar, that sort of wealth means lifelong material autonomy. Both Y and the Weaver were invited to attend the sabha. It was a big honour, and we could think of little else in the days that led up to it.

The site of Janak's sabha was a sangam, three free-flowing rivers braided into one. It was a special place where no distinction was made between material and spiritual, corporeal and intellectual.

Janak, presiding over the sabha, was that rarest of jewels – a leader of men who was powerful but kind, engaged while being detached. He was also a doting father to a baby girl he had found when he struck the earth with a plough.

Janak had once been Y's student, and each held the other in highest regard.

The debate began.

In that immense gathering of scholars and seekers who kowtowed to his great mind, it was Y's brilliant protege who made a bid to upstage her own teacher.

Y's face did not light up with joy at the challenge.

Janak was watching with rapt attention too. He knew the Weaver. She had been feted as one of the Nine Jewels of his court. She wore the title lightly.

The debate went on for hours. The Weaver's questions were bright, precise and unending. Y took them on with equal flair. Back-forth. Warp-weft. Point-counterpoint. Each answer he offered was scrutinised more and more closely.

What did they debate? The nature of this thing and that, this world and others, space and time – everything. She asked and he fielded. She probed, he relented. She persevered, he dug his heels in. She insisted, he bared his teeth. She jabbed, he hit back. She stung, he recoiled, then stung back.

We watched the aggression mount in their push-pull. Was this a clash of ideas or a clash of wills? Where were atman and brahman? Why this debate?

The audience began to get restless, but the debate continued.

We wandered away for lunch. I had brought with me neatly wrapped packets of food. Turned out they were enough to feed the multitudes. The ones who craved tangy found tamarind rice in their packet.

The king saw his flag as a symbol of peace. I saw predator and prey in unnatural proximity. When Janak was well fed, I gently pointed out how brutal the banner was. For the beasts to cohabit, instinct must be sedated, stomach amputated.

Wisdom, Janak said, isn't about discipline or submission. It is about letting your strength feed the hunger of the weak. The wisest of kings have indulged the cruellest gossip about their queens. Would you say it was fair to the queens?

Your questions enter dangerous territory. Careful, Weaver, lest your head falls off –
Ha ha ha!
This was't a personal threat. To seek the blade of truth is to permanently risk your head. Somewhere in the audience, the Ritualist laughed hard at the sight of Y rattled by a student who asked too many questions.
They could've had the most sparkling debate had either of them cared to listen.
They could have fed each other instead of behaving like predators.
Eventually, Y emerged triumphant, if tired.
I can't defeat you – yet.
I thought you wanted to learn.
And so King Janak's sabha was over.

LADLE

After King Janak's sabha, the fabric unravelled and the membranes ruptured. The Weaver was the first to leave the field, others would soon follow.

Y led the thousand gold-adorned cows to me. To him, this was an act that ensured I would always have milk and fuel, enough cows to trade or sell. I would not need to worry about material comforts again. I did not disagree.

There's enough here for two to eat en route –
How did you know I was leaving? How did you know I wouldn't leave alone?
Because you are not me.

Remember why we planted the banyan where we did?

It couldn't live in a courtyard or a grove without destroying all that was around it.

The field emptied out. I stayed put. The stillness didn't last long.

Sounds of the day caught up. Cows whose udders ached to be emptied, the tittering of children, the footfall of traders, wayfarers. And seekers.

<< From earth she learned patience. From wind, movement. From mountains, patience. From rivers, persistence. >>
<< From outstretched branches and deep roots, she understood hunger. >>
<< In every predator, she also saw frightened prey. She learned from butterflies how to gather without bruising another. >>

<< Aranya, says the Large, has no favourites. Constant taking, inadvertent giving. >>
<< She saw what no one else saw, the imagined hungers of the teacher, the Weaver and this Fig. >>
<< Says the Fig, I know so much more than before – from her field, her grove and her kitchen. >>

Who feeds the one who feeds everyone? I must return to hold the ladle to Katyayani's lip. Allow me to go, Y.
You will never need my permission to go, to grow –

As she walked away, the Fig, who had never worn any of her own garlands, tucked a flower behind her ear. She felt the stirring of urgent hunger.

MAKING ARANYAKA

Amruta's work table

WITHIN THIS DENSE FOREST, EVERY KNOWN DRAMA UNFOLDS

DEVDUTT

The title of this book, Aranyaka, meaning 'of the forest', alludes to a set of 3000-year-old Vedic scriptures full of mysterious metaphors, composed after the Samhitas (hymn collections), alongside the Brahmanas (ritual manuals), but before the Upanishads (philosophical expositions). This book is inspired not so much by these scriptures themselves as it is by the foundational role forests play in Vedic lore. Vedic thought is essentially about what it means to be cultured and civilised: the journey from hunger and fear, through domestication, towards empathy. I realised this after spending 20 years working with the Puranas (story chronicles) that have communicated Vedic lore for the past 2000 years.

AMRUTA

D met me in late 2016 with an A4-size printout with bullet points on it. Abstract themes ('Prey', 'Rivalry', 'Infinity', 'Zero', 'Dependant to Independent to Dependant') that he wanted to see as part of a book tentatively called 'A Vedic Truth'. It was, I will confess, a bit of a stretch to imagine all these transformed into a graphic novel.

D

The Vedas have always intrigued Indians. But what they actually say is highly contested. They are said to be 'not created by humans' (a-paurusheya). Most people assume this means something supernatural or divine. But it means exactly that: not human, wisdom from outside the human imagination (purusha), one that has always existed in nature (prakriti). The Rig Veda introduces us to Aranyani, the forest goddess (aranya being a forest 'that no one tills but still is full of food'). The Sama Veda divides all Vedic songs into 'melodies of the settlement' and 'melodies of the forest'. The Ramayana and the Mahabharata speak of the forest exile of princes who encounter sages and demons in the forest. The Puranas speak of various kinds of groves and forests inhabited by gods: the sugarcane forest of Ganesha, the cedar forest of Shiva, the tulsi grove of Krishna, the banana grove of Hanuman, the tamarind grove of Lakshmi.

Sanskrit texts refer to 'matsya nyaya' or the law of fishes, the Indian equivalent of the 'law of the jungle' as indicative of adharma (when humans submit to their animal behaviour – domination, territoriality, setting up a pecking order – society sees it as adharma). To overcome this, we need yagna, exchange based on empathy. Why yagna? Scholars have finally admitted that yagna is not some exotic mystical ritual but a pragmatic one: 'reciprocal exchange between humans and gods'. The exchange of goods and services is at the heart of human relationships and civilisation. It determines our humanity. Animals do not exchange, as humans do, voluntarily, creatively, by establishing value. Successful exchange happens only when we empathise with the needs of the other, hence the importance of seeing, or darshan. Yet, neither jungle law nor reciprocal exchange is central to the popular understanding of Vedic lore. Monastic themes such as the soul, autonomy and detachment dominate. This seems at odds with the celebration of colour, fragrance, taste, texture and rasa (aesthetic lifesap), to be found in Hindu temples. Forest, domestication, exchange, observation, body awareness: We had fragments, and I wanted to piece the puzzle together as a whole.

A

My life in rural France is a quiet one, with not much room for materialism. Observing the seasons, hours spent by the river watching a pair of swans raise their hatchlings, experiencing the hibernation of a long winter. I am an avid reader of nature writing and popular science. Authors like William Bryant Logan, David George Haskell or Sumana Roy often hit the same high notes as the best philosophical and spiritual writers, because observing the elements and the natural world transforms the way humans think.

Vedic sages knew this and placed great emphasis on such observation by sitting still (like hermits in termite mounds) or otherwise (forest exiles). I wanted readers to 'see' the way these sages did. Nothing unfolds in our tale that wouldn't organically emerge during observations of animal or plant behaviour. The forest here isn't romanticised – it is a place that is as unmaliciously violent as it is beautiful. The book refuses to let things enter the realm of abstruse. Scriptures are not – and should never be! – flash-frozen in some bygone era. They are being rewritten all the time. In a sense, that is what is happening here. It is an ambitious project.

OPEN-ENDED GARLAND OF IMAGES AND TEXT

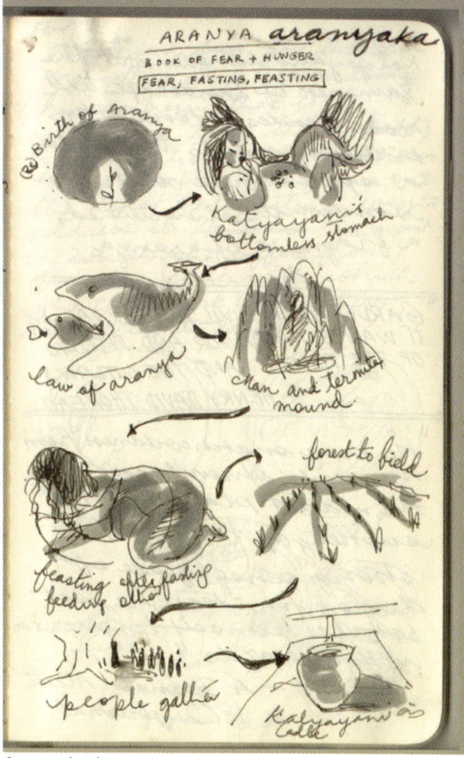

Concept sketches

D

Vedic ideas have been expressed differently over time. First they were oral and given form through fire rituals. Later they were more visual, as seen in temple culture. Technology is today widely used by Hindus as a part of worship – from apps that help you chant to livestreaming of temple rituals and weddings. I wanted us to present Vedic ideas using text and imagery, hence it had to be a graphic novel. I approached Amruta because I am a fan of her first graphic novel *Kari*, which made me deeply experience the love and loneliness of Indian urban life. We both wrote columns in the magazine *First City* for years, before we became friends at the first TED conference at Mysore in 2009. But it was only in 2016, when she was working on *Sauptik*, that I proposed we work together to create this book. I needed someone who was a seeker but not overwhelmed by tradition, someone with a mature but still-evolving personal style when it came to images and choice of words. Most importantly, I wanted a complementary point of view, a different expression, politics through aesthetics and compassion, not rage. Amruta was a clear choice.

A

After twenty years and fifty-odd books, D still gets so excited about a project at hand. He remains remarkably unjaded, and this brings a lot of energy to those he works with. One aspiration we have in common, which makes a lot of differences of opinion bridgeable, is a desire to *understand* the world rather than sit in judgement of it. There isn't much – whether profound, mundane or bawdy – I couldn't bring up in discussion with D. Which is just as well, because creating the book entailed a lot of talking through precisely such human preoccupations. This, a collaboration between two distinctly different but ready and willing individuals, was the only way a book about 'learning to see the other' could have been written.

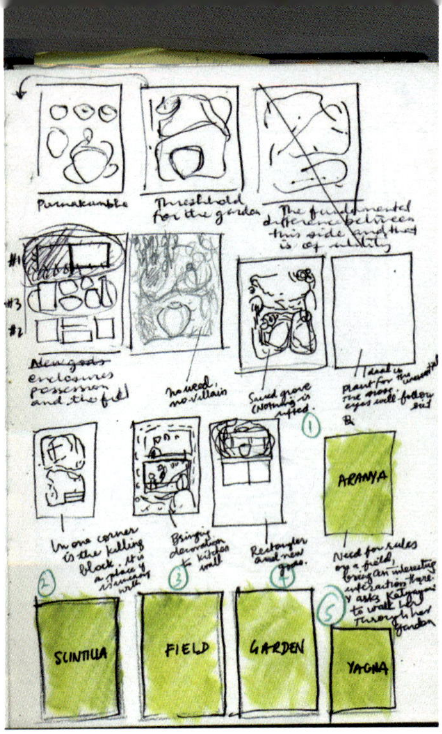

Planning the chapter breakdown

HE IS NOT ME SHE IS NOT ME

A

Role division was a big apprehension. We are both fairly controlling about our work turfs, even if our ways are very different. I feared that a clash of wills would hurt our friendship. Unexpectedly, I found that working with an independent-minded person meant that my own boundaries (and foibles) were understood intuitively. That both of us are aesthetes with a well-developed equation with text + image proved to be an advantage – D had no trouble understanding the visual grammar of the graphic novel or making the leap of imagination while looking at a rough drawing.

My table has always been a portable altar. And the year I created *Aranyaka*'s art, I rented a studio with a tangled, magical garden: a grove–oasis. Working in a highrise in a crowded metropolis could never have yielded the same result.

I have used opaque, heavy media like acrylics and collage in my previous two books. This one demanded a medium that was pellucid, light, non-toxic. So I chose watercolours and water-soluble pencils – my first time working with these media. It was great fun.

D

I was clear I wanted to function at a conceptual level only and leave Amruta to make the unmanifest manifest, from 'asat' to 'sat' as the Vedas say. We engaged intensely on every aspect – and I just loved how Amruta would plunge into botany, zoology, village art, kitchen engineering, pottery and weaving techniques to give thought a form. On WhatsApp I shared artworks that I felt might inspire her – my favourite depiction of a king on the walls of Khajuraho turned into her King Janak. She shared scribbles for me to comment on. I sometimes edited the text, or art, to include a Vedic phrase or symbol that had to be incepted without being obvious. But the final call was always Amruta's.

D

I know that collaboration is easier said than done. I give corporate workshops on this – how churning enables collaboration and how tug-of-war, argument, and words like 'pushback' are competitive and unnecessarily violent. Building on each other's ideas rather than simply agreeing or disagreeing needs genuine trust, respect and affection. I don't believe in the politically correct doctrine of 'equality' – for me we are all unique, and power has to be exchanged continuously, each one taking turns leading, knowing when to be silent and make room. Our conversations were often expressed using *Aranyaka*'s metaphor ('even the best peach trees cannot bring forth pears') as well as corporate jargon ('every plant and animal and human has SWOT: strength, weakness, opportunity, threat'). Unless we discovered each other's aranya, we would not be able to present it to the reader.

A

My second apprehension was a more uncomfortable personal one: how our collaboration would be perceived by others. Having written the text and designed the characters, I did not want to be seen as only an illustrator on the project. People are quick to project hierarchies and seed doubts. By now, D is a brand. And although I am no newbie, the 'risk' of his presence eclipsing mine (in their perception, not in his actions) is a real one. I dealt with this by being upfront about my insecurity – with myself and with D. To ask for rightful space and validation, to cede space and offer validation: this is integral to any skilful exchange. We surfaced from this in a way the scriptures would have approved of: with deepened trust and affection.

Character design for the Weaver

BRINGING TOGETHER KATYAYANI, Y, THE FIG AND THE WEAVER

Sangam of rivers

A

I suggested creating a parable – a love story maybe, or a story about rivalries or food – something disarmingly simple that you could finish reading without even realising you had just emerged from an immersive swim in Vedic ideas. The forest is a repeating motif in our lore, physically and metaphorically. And rather than being a 'savage' place, it is a site of profound personal and spiritual transformation.

As the story unfolds and characters reveal themselves, the habitats and colour palette of *Aranyaka* transform too. The bottle-green and burnt umber of the deep forest give way to the red ochre and burnt sienna of cleared field. This, in turn, gives way to the purple- and pink-inflected grove, and the crowds and bustle of Janak's sabha.

D

For me, the book was a set of concepts. No characters, no plots, no stories. Just a string of ideas. Amruta insisted on a story for ease of communication. When I overcame my initial hesitation about using a story, I loved the choice Amruta had made: the Upanishadic story of Yagnavalkya and his two wives, his debate with Gargi and conversations with Janak. But it bothered me that Katyayani was always seen as inferior because she chose material wealth (cows) over knowledge.

Could the story be retold, keeping in line the larger Vedic thought where deha or body is as important as the resident of the body, dehi (atman, brahman)? Where aranya plays a key role in the enquiries of the sages? We, as a people, are highly territorial about Upanishadic narratives, and violently puritanical. I felt we should avoid overt references to specific characters. They served only as slivers of inspiration. Beyond this, we were inventing our own story to communicate thoughts that predated the Upanishads.

D

In most stories, men are in the foreground and women in the background. We hear of Vedic rishikas but know very little about them. I liked the way Amruta gave them professions: potter, weaver, garland-maker. She spoke of the three rishikas coming together like *mukta veni* (free-flowing) rivers braiding together into a *yukta veni* (merged) river. She made the rishikas raw, elemental, worldly, part of a 'dog eat dog' world, not ethereal figures. The contrast between the village of rules where you are cared for and the uncaring forest of meritocracy, the Ritualist's ground and Janak's sabha, Y's classroom and Katyayani's kitchen, provided a vivid canvas for our characters. We wanted to show how rebellious students often become teachers who demand submission, and how vivaad (argument), as opposed to samvaad (dialogue), ends up becoming more about winning than learning.

A

The 'mainland India' hegemony in traditional representations of characters bores me.

I chose to represent Y as virile and hirsute, a lion among men, a far cry from the wispy rishis with long white Amar Chitra Katha beards. For the 'non-cerebral', instinct-led Katyayani, I gravitated towards the imagery of village goddesses, they of the staring eyes, and the goddess Aranyani, forest incarnate. Katyayani's abundance is physically manifest in her big hair, big body, big appetite, and her capacity to learn from everything she encounters – vegetable and romantic rival alike.

To emphasise the other-ness of those Katyayani learns to see, I chose a female cast that differed from her temperamentally and physically. The decision to go 'pan-Indian' with morphology is a very conscious one. Katyayani – sensuous, intuitive, plus-sized – has large Durga eyes and deep curves. The Fig – bright, non-competitive and keen to be seen for her mind, not body – has features that bring to mind the north-east of India or the high mountains. The Weaver – competitive, autonomous, led by reason – is lean, androgynous, and has dark skin.

Aranyaka WhatsApp discussions

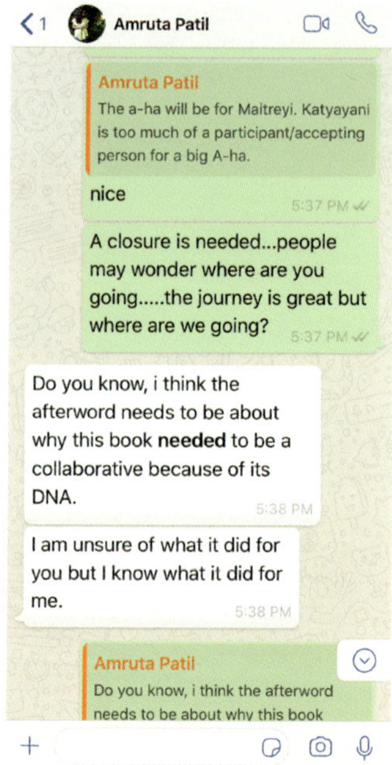

DO YOU SEE ME?

D

Collaborating long distance is not an easy thing. Amruta was in France and I was in India, but – aside from not being able to meet as often as we would have liked – we could have been anywhere and still worked this way. There were many hiccups, of course. Sometimes I felt we were going around in circles. I felt I failed at communicating ideas when Amruta would go back to traditional meanings ('yagna is a ritual'). We are conditioned to see gurus in a particular way – denied humanity, even though the Puranas are full of jealous, competitive and angry sages. Also, sometimes I felt we were grappling with too many ideas. Only when truly internalised would her art have the power to communicate.

A

D does not always realise how complex some of the themes he lives with can be for others. On an average morning, I'd wake up in my time zone 4.5 hours behind IST, to a cascade of voice messages on WhatsApp in response to things I had sent the night before. Things to reconsider, references to this statue or that essay. We pushed/pulled so often that those references (my love for the word 'scintilla', for example, or his knee-jerk response to the word 'gratitude') have become inside jokes. After several notebooks of scribbled notes, innumerable Skype calls, five hundred Post Its, and the most academic and relentless use of WhatsApp imaginable, I may be coming closer to understanding the idea of yagna.

Shalbhanjika from Sanchi. Image: WikiCommons

KEEPING THE REFERENCES DIVERSE

D

Aranyaka is littered with ideas from across the Vedic world. The idea that gods came later comes to us from the Creation Hymn of the Rig Veda. Food is central in the Vedas: the yagna is essentially an act of feeding the devas with ladles; the fire in the altar is the mouth of the gods. In the Taittriya Upanishads, we have brahman being described as both food (anna) and consumer of food (annada). Flesh (annakosha) is essentially food transformed, in yoga. In the Bhagavad Gita, brahman is seen in the one who feeds, the one who eats, in the ladle, the food, and the fire that digests the food. This is a popular Hindu prayer before mealtime. Unlike Christianity, where God is provider of food, for Hindus food itself is God; unlike in Islam, where God is outside humans, for Hindus God is within all organisms, awaiting realisation. In our book Ramayana's Sita, daughter of Janak, makes a special appearance. We mingle the Upanishadic story of Satyakama and his cows with the Puranic story of Dilip, who protects his cows from a lion in the story of Upakoshala. There is also a reference to Avadhuta Gita, the song of the mendicant who sees teachers everywhere in nature and culture.

A

In Nath literature, women who are potters, weavers and garland-makers are often seen as yoginis with magical powers, feared by hermits. Images connecting a woman's womb to a pot, and to the lotus, are widespread in subaltern art, and they trickle into *Aranyaka*'s imagery. Katyayani stands like a Shalbhanjika (a fertility motif in Buddhism, Jainism and Hinduism) or squats like Lajja Gauri. The Fig's songs are inspired by the works of Bahinabai, a Marathi bhakti poet, who used metaphors born of household chores. In the sabha chapter towards the end of the book, I was tickled to integrate a visual reference to the *wagh-bakri* (tiger and goat) logo of a popular tea brand into Janak's royal flag. The image happens to be popular in Indian folklore and mirrors the Biblical idea of the lion lying with the lamb in heaven.

A

As with my mythological graphic novel duology (*Adi Parva* and *Sauptik*), analogies and visual allusions in *Aranyaka* come from many sources. The flora and fauna shown on these pages aren't trying to accurately depict biodiversity in any specific part of the world. I have chosen to show insects, birds and flowers that best serve the accompanying text or colour palette. The black panther, Katyayani's 'wild' alter ego, is an ode to my fascination with the jaguars of Meso-American iconography. The image of Katyayani frolicking in a forest pool is an ode to the story of Leda and the Swan. There appears, too, an iconographical inversion of the Egyptian gods Nut and Geb. The audacious body language of the Weaver is based on the Dancing Girl statuette from Harappa. The Fig in her 'terrifying' form channelises Karaikal Ammaiyar (and other female bhaktas of that ilk) who laid waste to her own beautiful body so it would not distract from her spiritual potential. The text lovingly winks at references ranging from the Prajnaparamita Hridaya Sutra to Pupul Jayakar to Barbara Kingsolver to anonymous Chinese proverbs (Confucious? 🙂). The only thing that matters is that I retain fidelity to the essence.

D

Amruta was most excited when I told her the concept of a-surya-sparsha, a much desired princess untouched by the sun, and of Karaikal Ammaiyar, who makes herself ugly in her quest to avoid the world of men and find God. These influenced the character development of the Fig. The sage in the termite hill is a recurring motif in the Puranas; a visual indicator of one who has conquered the sense organs. We used it to introduce Y. The Kumbha Mela of Prayag, where three rivers meet, inspired the location of Janak's sabha. It is here that Hindu mendicants meet to catch up and discuss philosophy and settle disputes. They are not just pot-smoking naked mendicants bathing in the waters, as the Western media projects them to enthral New Age spiritual wannabies.

Karaikal Ammaiyar. Image: WikiCommons

Character design for the Fig

MAKING 'ENORMOUS' ACCESSIBLE

A

I think we have accomplished our goal of creating a complex story that is 'disarmingly simple'. There is a lot going on if you care to see. Beneath its surface are many narrative undercurrents – the ecological one, the feminist one, the one where food is really a stand-in for many other sorts of human appetites. *Aranyaka*'s women shine in the classroom (there is no gendering the mind!) and its men work a grinding stone, play with babies, and shed a tear. None of these details are heavy-handed. Food fundamentalism, body and sex-positivity are all addressed with a light touch. There is the diversity in body type and skin colour I spoke of earlier; there is, too, a glad-hearted celebration of hairy chests on men; unibrow, frizzy hair and unwaxed armpits in women.

All that said, D and I are wary of the tyranny of political correctness (almost as bullying as the tyranny of bigots) which allows a narrative to be addressed only in a specific way in order for it to pass muster. Speak from another slant, and you risk being ostracised.

D

I was a little scared of talking too much about sex and non-vegetarian food as Hindus are becoming increasingly intolerant, disagreeing aggressively with the suggestion that sages did not see sex as 'sin' and did not just eat roots and shoots. I requested Amruta to tone these ideas down and she agreed (though there were tense moments over the stifling of artistic liberty). We did not want the larger idea to be derailed by immature trolls.

THE WARP OF OUR STORIES HAS ALWAYS BEEN HUNGER

Gestures of protection and providing. Image: WikiCommons

D

A

Our ancient stories and visual traditions continually remind us of the elements, of wilderness and our fellow sentient creatures, of our agrarian roots and of the human being's place amidst (not atop) that schema. In stark contrast, urban India has an acute nature deficit disorder and frightening delusions that there are infinite resources to meet infinite greed. Neither river nor soil nor seed nor bird nor beast figure in most people's imaginations, except in the form of tapped water, caricatured animals in cartoons or the occasional pet dog or potted plant. To be divorced from nature is to be divorced from Vedic thought. To put aranya back in people's consciousness seemed like an urgent responsibility at this time in our collective history. I see this as 'earthing' and 'grounding' in their truest sense.

Gestures indicating protection (from fear) and providing (for hunger) are a constant feature in Hindu iconography. From an evolutionary point of view, these are primal sensations that separate the living from the non-living. I realised we are driven by hunger and fear just as dinosaurs were millions of years ago. I have seen the power of these ideas in my lectures and workshops in colleges, schools and corporate houses. I myself have become a kinder and more forgiving person since I was able to better see the insecurities and frailties that underlie human decision-making. I have seen the arrogance of gurus who chuckle to hide their fears. I have seen fabulously wealthy people terrified of exile, loneliness and poverty. I am convinced that this is at the heart of Vedic lore – an understanding of the other, the complexity of human relationships, and our imagined fears that make us take refuge in our animal nature. Of course, I could be wrong. Hence I always begin my books, and conclude this one, with the following lines:

Within infinite myths lies an eternal truth
Who sees it all?
Varuna has but a thousand eyes
Indra, a hundred
You and I, only two.

INDEX
OF VEDIC CONCEPTS

(Sanskrit and Hindi words that inspired every page in *Aranyaka*)

CONCEPTS

Page 17	Prakriti (nature)
Page 18	Bhakti (surrender)
Page 19	Udaseen (indifferent)
Page 20	Kshudha (hunger); Trishna (thirst)
Page 21	Rati (sex); Yoni (womb, space of reproduction)
Page 22	Kula (clan, herd, pack, hive)
Page 23	Bechara (helpless, without fodder, victim); Vira (hero, he who fights back)
Page 24	Pashu bali (sacrifice of animals)
Page 25	Vana devi (forest goddess)
Page 26	Para (other); Param (infinite other)
Page 27	Buddhi (intelligence, ability to evaluate)
Page 28	Drishti (observe); Kavacha (armour)
Page 29	Sahachara (companion)
Page 30	Ahuti (offering)
Page 31	Bandhu (friendship)
Page 32	Nidhi (treasure, hoard)
Page 33	Mukta (unattached)
Page 34	Shalabhanjika (tree nymph); Tapasvi (ascetic)
Page 35	Sankalpa (declaration of intent); Svaha (offering); Tathastu (receivable)
Page 36	Bhoga (satisfaction of hungers)
Page 37	Dravya sharira (body); Bhava sharira (mind)
Page 38	Yagna (feeding the gods)
Page 39	Pancha yagna (feeding the other)
Page 40	Yajur Veda
Page 41	Adi guru (primal teacher)
Page 42	Ahimsa (non-violence)
Page 43	Anekanta-vaad (diversity of thought)
Page 44	Kama (desire)

ACKNOWLEDGEMENTS

Arun and Alka, for instilling an early love of the forest. Anaël, for an instinctively harmonious connection with nature and beauty – *I learned so much with you*. P, for introducing me to a Vedic home many years ago. Nour, Adaleta, Cynthia, Amrita and Ahmad for unflinching conversations about human fears and hungers. Pili and Brigitte for being there, solidly.

For his 10th birthday, this book is a gift to Neel Patil.

This project was supported by La Maison des Auteurs and La Cité internationale de la bande dessinée et de l'image (Angoulême, France).

Amruta Patil
September 2019

SUGGESTED READING

- C. Rajagopalachari, *Upanishads* (Bhartiya Vidya Bhavan).
- Ed. Gavin Flood, *The Blackwell Companion to Hinduism*, 2005 (Wiley-Blackwell).
- Alf Hiltebeitel, *Dharma: Dimensions of Asian Spirituality*, 2010 (University of Hawaii Press), Kindle Edition.
- Frits Staal, *Discovering the Vedas: Origins, Mantras, Rituals, Insight*, 2009 (Penguin Global).
- S.W Jamison and M. Witzel, *Vedic Hinduism*, 1992 (Harvard University Press).
- Patrick Olivelle, *The Early Upanishads: Annotated Text and Translation*, 1996 (OUP).
- Devdutt Pattanaik, *My Gita*, 2015 (Rupa Publications).
- Bahinabai Chaudhari, *Bahinabainchi Gani* (Suchitra Prakashan).
- Pupul Jayakar, *The Earth Mother: Legends, Goddesses and Ritual Arts of India*, 1990 (HarperCollins).
- Roberto Calasso, *Ardor*, 2015 (Penguin).
- Sudhakshina Rangaswami, *The Roots of Vedanta: Selections from Sankara's Writing*, 2012 (Penguin).
- David George Haskell, *The Forest Unseen: A Year's Watch in Nature*, 2013 (Penguin USA).
- Peter Wohlleben, *The Hidden Life of Trees: What They Feel, How They Communicate*, 2016 (Penguin Random House India).
- Barbara Kingsolver, *Animal, Vegetable, Miracle: Our Year of Seasonal Eating*, 2008 (Faber & Faber).
- Samin Nosrat, *Salt Fat Acid Heat: Mastering the Elements of Good Cooking*, 2017 (Simon & Schuster).
- Vandana Shiva, *Staying Alive: Women, Ecology and Survival in India*, 2009 (Women Unlimited).
- Alan W. Watts, *Nature, Man and Woman*, 1991 (Vintage).

ALSO BY AMRUTA PATIL

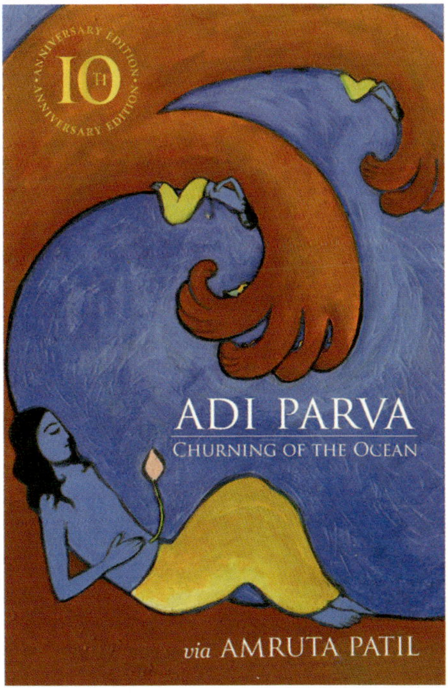

30 Years *of*

HarperCollins *Publishers* India

At HarperCollins, we believe in telling the best stories and finding the widest possible readership for our books in every format possible. We started publishing 30 years ago; a great deal has changed since then, but what has remained constant is the passion with which our authors write their books, the love with which readers receive them, and the sheer joy and excitement that we as publishers feel in being a part of the publishing process.

Over the years, we've had the pleasure of publishing some of the finest writing from the subcontinent and around the world, and some of the biggest bestsellers in India's publishing history. Our books and authors have won a phenomenal range of awards, and we ourselves have been named Publisher of the Year the greatest number of times. But nothing has meant more to us than the fact that millions of people have read the books we published, and somewhere, a book of ours might have made a difference.

As we step into our fourth decade, we go back to that one word – a word which has been a driving force for us all these years.

Read.

Harper Collins · 4th · HARPER PERENNIAL · HARPER BUSINESS · HARPER BLACK · हार्पर हिन्दी

HarperCollins *Children's Books* · HARPER DESIGN · HARPER VANTAGE · Harper Sport